WHEN YOU FAIL

Buster's Ears Trip Him Up

EDWARD T. WELCH

Editor

JOE HOX

Illustrator

Story creation by Jocelyn Flenders, a homeschooling mother, writer, and editor living in suburban Philadelphia. A graduate of Lancaster Bible College with a background in intercultural studies and counseling, the Good News for Little Hearts series is her first published work for children.

New Growth Press, Greensboro, NC 27404
Text copyright © 2018 by Edward T. Welch
Illustration copyright © 2018 by New Growth Press

Cover/Interior Design and Typesetting: Trish Mahoney, themahoney.com
Cover/Interior Illustrations: Joe Hox, joehox.com

ISBN: 978-1-948130-25-7

Library of Congress Cataloging-in-Publication Data
Names: Welch, Edward T., 1953- author.
Title: Buster's ears trip him up : when you fail / Edward T. Welch.
Description: Greensboro : New Growth Press, 2018. | Series: Good news for
  little hearts
Identifiers: LCCN 2018043744 | ISBN 9781948130257 (trade cloth)
Subjects: LCSH: Failure (Psychology)--Religious
  aspects--Christianity--Juvenile literature.
Classification: LCC BT730.5 .W45 2018 | DDC 242/.62--dc23
LC record available at https://lccn.loc.gov/2018043744

Printed in Malaysia

25 24 23 22 21 20 19 18   2 3 4 5 6

"'But God showed his great love for us by sending Christ to die for us while we were still sinners."

Romans 5:8

Just beyond Mulberry Meadow,
in a pleasant little burrow, lived Papa, Mama, Ivy, and Buster Bunny. Their hidden lair—
with its secret nooks and crawlways—was the perfect hideaway for their family.

At dawn, sunbeams trickled down into the burrow, warming the air. Mama and Papa sat sipping their cups of clover tea in the kitchen.

Everything was quiet and peaceful.

And then the floorboards thundered as Buster came darting and dashing down the tunnel from his bedroom to the kitchen. He was always in a hurry—always in a race to be first.

As he rushed into the kitchen, he said,
"Good morning!
I'm all packed and ready for camp!"

Papa replied, "That's great, Buster! What's your rush? "

Buster replied, "I want to get there early to practice for
the big race! Practice makes perfect, right Papa?"

Papa replied, "Well it certainly helps.
So you think you'll win again this year, do you?"

Buster said,
"I sure do!
I'm the fastest bunny
in the meadow!"

Ivy entered the kitchen and replied,
"I'm sure you'll run fast, Buster!
You always do. But does winning really matter that much?"

Buster never heard Ivy's question—he was too busy
imagining Miss Parker, the camp director, handing him a trophy.
He could even hear the loud applause of the crowd!
The only thing keeping him from that trophy was breakfast.
He turned to Mama, "May I have breakfast? I have to get going!"

Mama smiled and set a delicious spread of
green-grass juice and fresh wildflowers on the table.

And then she prayed,
"Thank you, Father, for the food on our table.
And thank you for Camp Greenwood.
Thank you for being there with Ivy and Buster,
and also for being with Papa and me.
Help us each to know you better this week. Amen."

After enjoying their breakfast, Buster and Ivy washed their dishes and grabbed their bags. Papa turned to Buster, handed him a little folded note and said, "You'll know the right time to read this."

Then he hugged them, "We love you both! Have a great week!"

The bunnies hopped up the burrow hole and
above ground. It was a beautiful day! The robins were
caroling, the chipmunks were chattering, and the squirrels
were scampering from branch to branch.
The forest was full of life!

As Buster and Ivy hopped down the path,
they recalled their favorite camp memories—
the familiar songs and friends, the crafts and games,
the meals—and of course, the big race.

Ivy said, "I can't wait to get there!"

Before long, they saw the welcome
sign nestled within the thicket.

Together they shouted,
"CAMP
GREENWOOD!"
and raced ahead.

Miss Parker waved and exclaimed, "Welcome, Ivy and Buster! I'm so glad to see you!
Ivy, you're going to absolutely love this year's activities, especially the nature crafts.
And, Buster, I'd imagine you're excited for this year's race! Everyone remembers how
fast you were last year! I think your cabin will be glad to have a bunny like you!"

Buster declared, "Thank you, Miss Parker. I'm even faster than I was last year!"
Buster ran to the meadow to practice his running. The big race was the next day!

Before dawn, Buster was up and ready for the day.
As soon as he heard the breakfast bell clang,
he rushed out of the cabin and ran down the path.

"Practice makes perfect,
practice makes perfect," he repeated.

His friend, Henry Hedgehog,
trailed behind him.

Henry, trying to catch his breath, exclaimed,
"Buster! Our cabin will surely win the race with you on our side!"
Buster agreed. "I certainly am the fastest!"

The campers lined up in the big meadow according to their cabins, and Miss Parker excitedly announced, "Good morning, Camp Greenwood! Please listen carefully. Each camper will run up and back. Once you've had your turn, sit down in your line. The first cabin to finish the race wins! Have fun!"
Buster was racing last for his cabin.

"We are sure to win if I'm running last," he said to Henry. "Even if we are behind when I start, I'll be able to get ahead!"

Each camper, with rapidly beating hearts, stood in position. Miss Parker raised the bullhorn and yelled, "On your mark, get set, GO!"

The field became a flurry of activity, with animals racing
across the meadow and back. One by one,
Buster's teammates slid back in line.

He was next. As soon as Henry tagged Buster, he bolted onto the field, flying as
fast as ever! He was already thinking about holding that trophy.

As Buster's feet pounced and his heart thumped,
his ears flopped furiously in the wind.

Just as he pulled ahead of Freddie Fox,
he turned to see how far behind everyone else was.
His ears swung around with his head.

Suddenly one of his ears
flipped back and planted itself
across his eyes like a blindfold.

He could not get it off and
everything went black.

Within seconds, Buster
TRIPPED,
       TUMBLED, and
           TOPPLED onto the ground.

Everything went silent and everyone stopped to stare. Some even laughed.
Buster felt sick to his stomach. His face turned red. He was embarrassed from
his head to his toes. He remembered how he told everyone how fast
he was—how he'd surely win the race. What would they think of him now?
The weight of it all seemed to hold him down. He could not get up.

Miss Parker rushed to his side
and asked,
"Buster, are you okay?"
Buster looked up through
tear-filled eyes.

Ivy ran to Buster and helped him up. Miss Parker whispered to Ivy,
"Why don't you and Buster take a little walk together?"

Ivy nodded and guided Buster into the woods next to the meadow.
Buster fixed his eyes on the leaves and twigs of the forest floor—never lifting his gaze.
Ivy put her arm around him and took a deep breath.

He looked so different—so defeated.
Ivy had never seen him like this.

She said, "Buster, I am so sorry that you fell."

Buster wiped a tear from his eyes and cried, "I was going to win! And then everyone saw me trip! I want to go home."

Ivy continued, "It doesn't matter to me whether or not you won the race. I'm your sister, and I will always love you. Winning or losing a race isn't the most important thing. The important thing is that you are still loved by Jesus. And his love never fails."

Buster said, "But what about my friends? How will I face them after telling them all week how fast I am?"

"Buster, remember when I gave a report about the wrong flower? Miss Minnick told the class I was going to talk about pansies, but I had studied petunias. I was so upset.

"I had no idea how I could ever face my classmates again. Every now and then, I think back and still feel sad about it. But no matter how many times I fail, God's love never fails. He always helps. The Great Book says that God takes care of those who fall. I know this is true."

Buster looked up and said, "I remember when that happened. You were upset about what your friends would think too."

"Yes," said Ivy. "I always thought I was the smartest in our class—and I told that to other people too. But you know that the Great Book says, 'pride goes before a fall.' Pride means that we think we are better than everyone. I was thinking I was the smartest—that was my pride and that's what really tripped me up. But you know what else the Great Book says?"

"What?" said Buster, he was listening intently now.

"It says that there is help for everyone who knows that they need help. God calls that being humble," said Ivy. "Sometimes we have to fail before we realize how much we need God's help. I told Jesus I was sorry for acting like I was better than my friends, and I know he forgave me."

Buster remembered the note from Papa. He reached into his pocket,
unfolded the piece of paper, and read out loud,

Remember - God loved you
before you ever did anything
right before you ever
reached a finish line.
   The Great Book says, But here
is how God has shown his love
for us. While we were still sinners
Christ died for us.
Love you, Buster.   Papa

Ivy smiled. "That's true!" she said. "Before you did anything right, God loved you.
God doesn't love you because you win a race. He loves you because you belong to him.
And he is always ready to forgive when our pride trips us up. Papa always says,
'You don't have to be the best, just try your best.' When we want everyone to think we are
the best that means we are only thinking about ourselves. That will really trip us up!"

Then Ivy asked,
"Are you ready to head back to camp?"

Buster smiled and said,
"Okay, Ivy. But can you pray for me first?"

"I'd love to," she said.
"Father, you are so kind. Thank you for using this race to show
us that we always need your help. Thank you for forgiving all
of our sin and mistakes. Help us to love others and not think
so much about ourselves. Amen."

Buster said, "I guess that practice won't ever make me perfect. Only Jesus is always perfect. I think he can even help me face my friends after falling flat on my face."

Ivy and Buster returned to the camp. As soon as he saw Buster, Henry Hedgehog ran up to him.

"That was epic.
That's one race we will never forget!"

Then he put his arm around Buster.
"Why don't you come and have an ice cream sundae with the rest of us!"

"Thanks, Henry."
Buster quickly hopped over to the ice cream—
with Henry again trailing behind.

Before long, Buster was laughing,
jumping, and even telling the story
of his epic fall.

Helping Your Child with Failure

How can you help your child with failure? One of the best ways is to let them see how you are growing in this area. You've probably already noticed that this problem does not disappear as you get older. It takes hold even more. But what if résumés, achievements, reputation, the approval of others, and the quest to be remembered were less important to you?

Imagine having nothing to hide in your closest relationships and being free to admit weakness and ask for help. Imagine a world where you are no longer ruled by the opinions of others. You would be affected by their opinions, either hurt or encouraged by them—there is no way around that. But you wouldn't be controlled by them. Instead, you would remember that everyone is better at some things than others and that failure is essential to learning and growing. This is not an imaginary world; it's God's world, and he invites each of us to live there with him. The alternative is a life prone to judging and being judged (they go together), anger, depression, and always trying to cover up and hide from others.

You can grow in trusting God when you fail, and as you do so, you can point your child to Jesus, who is an ever-present help in all kinds of trouble. Here are some things to talk over with your child that will point both of you to Jesus in the midst of failure.

1 **Failure is hard, but Jesus will help.** It's hard to try your best and still not achieve your goal. It's hard to fail in front of others. But failure is also an opportunity to grow. We might fail, but God's love never fails (Lamentations 3:22). We can go to Jesus for help in all of the hard moments of life (Hebrews 4:14–16).

2 **Having the wrong goal will trip us up.** Buster said that "practice makes perfect." But Buster wanted to be more than perfect; he wanted to be the best. He found out that having this goal did trip him up. It is not the answer to his, yours, or your child's struggle with identity and self-esteem because it is based on what we can do and what others think about what we do.

3 **Being "the best" versus "trying your best."** Ivy reminded Buster that Papa didn't tell them to be the best, but to try their best. The Bible says that we work, even for others "with a sincere heart, as you would Christ, not by the way of eye-service, as people-pleasers, but as bondservants of Christ, doing the will of God from the heart" (Ephesians 6:5–6 ESV). Work as if you were working for the Lord because you are. It's great to want to do your best, but motivation is key. We should want to work hard and have a good reputation *for the Lord's sake*.

4 **The problem is pride.** We want other people to look up to us for our sake, and we want to have our failures well-hidden so others don't look down on us. We want to be above others. And since that is not where God wants us to be, the proud will always teeter and fall, perhaps landing among the wise who are more familiar with weakness than strength. Here is how the Bible puts it, "If you are proud, you will be destroyed. If you are proud, you will fall" (Proverbs 16:18 NIRV).

5   **A simple prayer of confession to Jesus is a good way to come down from our perch.** The goal is to come down before we fall down. Once down, rejection can still hurt deeply, but when we don't live for the praise of other people, we can turn to Jesus and begin to see how God's world (the real world) is constructed differently (1 John 1:9–10).

6   **As we follow Jesus, we learn that life is not about living for our own glory.** The better we get to know Jesus, the less we think of our achievements. We realize that they are not enough to earn us the forgiveness and life forever that Jesus freely offers those who ask. When we realize that we have nothing of worth to bring to Jesus, this pleases and honors him. Then we can say to Jesus, "only you have what I truly need." To which we might add, "and it sure would be nice if you could help me think less often about myself." This is the path of true honor.

7   **God's kingdom is where we experience the best life.** Jesus came into this world and was determined to set it right. He ate with people who hurt his reputation, washed people's feet as their servant, and was penniless when he died. He was the King of the universe yet was looked down upon by the entire world, both Jews and Gentiles. But this was also the path to true glory. Jesus lived to glorify his heavenly Father and now he reigns forever as our risen Savior. As we lose things (like our reputation, others' good opinion of us, being "the best"), we find out that they were really getting in the way of the best things in life—knowing God's love, loving God, and loving people.

8   **Here are some Bible verses to share with your children when they experience failure.** They are also printed on the back tear-out page. Post them in your house or give them to your children to keep in their back pocket.

> *I waited patiently for the LORD to help me,*
> *   and he turned to me and heard my cry.*
> *He lifted me out of the pit of despair,*
> *   out of the mud and the mire.*
> *He set my feet on solid ground*
> *   and steadied me as I walked along.*
> *(Psalm 40:1–2)*

> *God opposes the proud*
> *   but gives grace to the humble.*
> *(James 4:6)*

> *But God showed his great love for us by sending Christ to die for us while we were still sinners. (Romans 5:8)*

> *So then, since we have a great High Priest who has entered heaven, Jesus the Son of God, let us hold firmly to what we believe. This High Priest of ours understands our weaknesses, for he faced all of the same testings we do, yet he did not sin. So let us come boldly to the throne of our gracious God. There we will receive his mercy, and we will find grace to help us when we need it most. (Hebrews 4:14–16)*

Back Pocket Bible Verses

I waited patiently for the Lord to help me,
and he turned to me and heard my cry.
He lifted me out of the pit of despair,
out of the mud and the mire.
He set my feet on solid ground
and steadied me as I walked along.

Psalm 40:1-2

God opposes the proud
but gives grace to the humble.

James 4:6

But God showed his great love for us
by sending Christ to die for us while
we were still sinners.

Romans 5:8

This High Priest of ours [Jesus]
understands our weaknesses, for he
faced all of the same testings we do,
yet he did not sin. So let us come
boldly to the throne of our gracious
God. There we will receive his mercy,
and we will find grace to help us
when we need it most.

Hebrews 4:15-16

Back Pocket Bible Verses

WHEN YOU FAIL

WHEN YOU FAIL

GOOD NEWS FOR LITTLE HEARTS

GOOD NEWS FOR LITTLE HEARTS

WHEN YOU FAIL

WHEN YOU FAIL

GOOD NEWS FOR LITTLE HEARTS

GOOD NEWS FOR LITTLE HEARTS